# All Year Round

A journey through the year ...

**Kane Miller**
A DIVISION OF EDC PUBLISHING

# Days of the Week

A **day** starts at midnight and ends the following midnight, **24 hours** later. Seven days in a row make up a **week**.

... followed by **Wednesday** ...

... and **Thursday!**

Next is **Friday.**

**Saturday** is the last day of the week! Saturday and Sunday are sometimes grouped together and called the **weekend.**

Can you write all the days of the week?

There are lots of things to do in a week.

On **Sunday**,
we go to the park.

The bus takes me to school on **Monday**.

I help my mom take the dog for a walk on **Tuesday**.

I like **Wednesday** because we have art class.

Every **Thursday**, I play soccer after school.

I spend **Friday** evenings with my grandparents.

Sometimes on **Saturday** we go someplace special.
I like when we visit the museum the best.

What about you?
What is your favorite thing to do each week?

# Months of the Year

There are **12 months** in the **year** and they always follow the same order.

Each month is either 30 or 31 days long, except February. February is usually 28 days, but every four years it is 29 days long instead. The year this happens is called a **leap year**.

# Seasons

We group the months together into four **seasons**: winter, spring, summer, and fall.
In many places, the year starts and ends in winter.

The **winter** months are colder.

*December, January, February*

In **spring**, plants start to grow.

*March, April, May*

**Summer** is hotter.

*June, July, August*

Many leaves change color in the **fall**.

*September, October, November*

# Calendar

We count off the days, weeks, and months of the year on a **calendar**. The calendar's columns usually go from Sunday to Saturday and the different rows show each new week. We can write down special days on the calendar to remember them.

My favorite month is **January**. It's the first
month of the year and everything is fresh and new.

In January, it is **winter**. I like winter because sometimes it snows
and my brothers and I make a HUGE snowman!

Does it snow where you live?

At the start of January, we might make **resolutions** for the new year. A resolution is a promise you make to yourself. Last year my resolution was to learn how to ride a bike.

What resolution would you make?

**Martin Luther King Jr. Day** is in January.
Martin Luther King Jr. was a leader in the civil rights movement and worked hard to make life fairer for Black Americans. We celebrate his achievements every year with a holiday and parades.

**February** is the second and shortest month in the year.

February 14th is **Valentine's Day** — when we tell the people we love how much they mean to us. I make cards for my abuela and my older sister.

Who do you celebrate on Valentine's Day?

**March** is the third month and the start of **spring**.
The weather becomes warmer, but I still need to wear my coat.

It is my birthday in March.
Every year, my dad makes
me a **BIG** chocolate cake.
My job is to lick the spoon!

When is
your birthday?

After March comes **April**, the fourth month.
I love April because everything is so green!

I help my mom in the garden.
We plant carrots, beets,
and peas.

Later in the year, we'll
pick them to eat.

I like visiting the park in April because
there are baby ducklings at the pond.

Lots of animals give birth
in spring and the world feels full of life!

What do you like about spring?

**May** is the fifth month.

In May, we celebrate **Mother's Day**.
I make my mom breakfast — it can get
a bit messy! Later, we read lots of books
together and then play a game.

The last Monday in May
is **Memorial Day**. We remember
all the brave people who have died
serving in the armed forces.

**June** is the sixth month. We're halfway through the year and it is now **summer**. June 19th is **Juneteenth**. It marks the day when the end of slavery was announced in Texas in 1865, and the whole country became free.

We spend the day with friends and family.

In June, it's **Father's Day**. I draw a picture for my dad and then we go bowling. I like being on my dad's team!

Do you do anything special in May or June?

Next comes **July**, which is the seventh month. July 4th is **Independence Day**. This holiday celebrates when America became its own country, separate from Great Britain. It's like a birthday for the USA!

Where I live, a big carnival comes to town. In the evening there is a concert with singing and lots of fireworks!

Do you do anything to celebrate Independence Day?

**August** is the eighth month. I love August because we go on vacation. I eat a lot of ice cream and build the best sandcastles.

What do you do in the summer?

**September** is the ninth month and the beginning of **fall**. The leaves change color and start to drop off the trees. I like to run through them and hear them CRUNCH!

The first Monday in September is **Labor Day**, which recognizes the importance of workers in our country. On Labor Day, I watch the parade and then go apple picking.

In September, we go back to school after summer vacation. I like seeing all my friends again.

What do you like about September?

The tenth month of the year is **October**.
October 31ˢᵗ is **Halloween**. My parents
help us carve pumpkins and put up spooky
decorations around the house.

Later, we put on costumes and go **trick-or-treating**.
This year I'm a dinosaur! Do you do anything to celebrate Halloween?

It's the eleventh month, **November**, and almost the end of the year! November 11th is **Veterans Day**. It is a holiday to say thank you to everyone in the armed forces.

The fourth Thursday in November is **Thanksgiving**. We have a big family meal. Before we eat, we each say what we've been thankful for this year.

What are you thankful for?

**December** is the twelfth and last month in the year! December 31st is **New Year's Eve**.
I stay up REALLY late and we count down to midnight.

3, 2, 1 ...

The new year has begun!

Now it's your turn … What do you do each week?
Draw or write your routine below.

Sunday

Monday

Tuesday

Wednesday

Thursday

Friday

Saturday